Why Is The Day All Gray?

It was a chilly morning in the Hundred-Acre Wood when Pooh and Roo arrived at Owl's house.

"Why is the day all gray?" asked Roo.

"The sun is hiding behind these low-hanging clouds," said Owl. "And this won't do at all."

"Why not?" asked Roo. "What's the matter?"

"The fog is the matter," Owl replied. "I simply cannot fly today. And I must get to my uncle's 'Who's Whooo?' party."

"Oh, dear," said Pooh. "When will the fog go away so that you can fly?"
"I don't know," Owl said sadly. "But I'm already late!"
"Maybe you could fly *through* the fog," suggested Pooh.

"No, no, no," said Owl. "That's impossible. This particular fog is much too thick and far too low for me to fly through. Why, I can't even see the next tree over."

"What is fog, anyway?" asked Roo.

Owl thought for a moment. "Fog," he began, "is like a cloud that hugs the ground."

"Oh," said Roo. "Well, when someone is hugging me too tightly, I push them away, like this!" Roo gave Pooh a gentle push.

"Perhaps we can *push* the fog out of the way for you," Pooh suggested.

"Let's try," said Roo excitedly.

Roo and Pooh pushed and pushed at the thick, damp air, but since there was only air to push against, the fog stayed right where it was. "Oh, bother," said Pooh. "It's still here."

"I guess my idea didn't work," said Roo. "Maybe the fog is only hugging *your* tree, Owl. Let's see if we can find a place in the Wood that isn't foggy."

"Splendid suggestion," said Owl.

The three friends walked through the Wood looking for a bright, sunny spot.

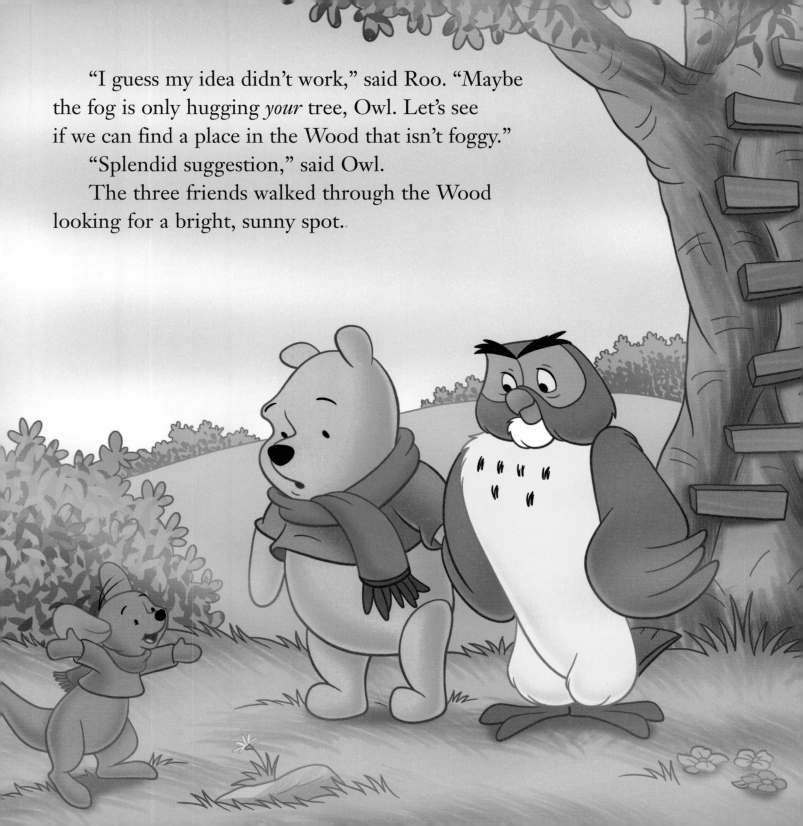

They soon saw a shadowy figure bounce by.

"Hoo-hoo-hoo!" cried Tigger. "Say, Beak Lips, what are you doin' walkin' when you got all those feathery things for flyin'?"

"It is my considered opinion that it is far too foggy to fly," said Owl.
"Tigger, can you help us make the fog go away so that Owl can fly?"
asked Roo.

Tigger thought for a moment. "Absotively!" he announced. "Getting rid of fog is what tiggers do best! I'll just give it a little scare and bouncity bounce the fog right back into the sky."

And so, Tigger crouched down low and popped up with a giant BOO! Then he booed and bounced all around. But the fog stayed right where it was.

Finally, Tigger stopped.

"Whew," said Tigger, shaking himself off. "Tryin' ta scare that fog away made me one soggy tigger."

"But it isn't raining," said Roo. "Where's the water coming from?"

"It must be in the fog," said Tigger, "'cause I'm absotively wet! Can't you feel it, Little Buddy?"

Roo lifted up his head and felt the cool, moist air on his face. The day was still gray and foggy.

"I'm sorry, Owl," said Roo. "The fog is everywhere. We just don't know how to make it go away."

"Perhaps Piglet will know," said Pooh. "He's always good with a puzzle."

"Great idea, Pooh Boy," said Tigger.

As the friends set off for Piglet's house, they couldn't see very well. Pooh and Roo went one way, while Owl and Tigger went another.

Suddenly, Roo heard a strange rustling sound. He hopped into Pooh's arms.

"What was that?" asked Roo.

"I don't know," said Pooh nervously. "It's really hard to see in all this fog."

Meanwhile, Tigger could not find Owl anywhere. Then, he started hearing strange sounds, too.

"Maybe if I disguiserize myself, whatever is making those scaredy sounds won't notice me," he thought.

Pooh kept walking until he bumped into something that looked like a striped tree.

"Tigger?" said Pooh.

"Hoo-hoo-hoo," laughed Tigger. "I'm sure glad it's you, Buddy Bear!"

The three friends kept walking until they got to Pooh's Thinking Spot. There, by the tree, they saw two lights shining through the fog.

"Wha-wha-what's that, Buddy Boys?" cried Tigger. "Let's get outta here!"

"I say," said a familiar voice. "It's about time you showed up."

"It's Owl!" cried Roo.

"Well, of course, it's me," said Owl. "I've been waiting for you."

Pooh looked up and noticed that a little breeze had blown some of the fog away.

"It's a little less foggy," he said. "Perhaps now would be a good time to look for Piglet's house."

Everyone agreed. They left Pooh's Thinking Spot, which Tigger renamed "Pooh's Scaredy Spot."

When the friends got to Piglet's house, they found him sweeping his walk.

"Hello, Piglet," said Roo. "Do you know how to get rid of this fog so that Owl can fly?"

"Oh, dear," said Piglet as he kept sweeping. "No, I don't."

"Wait!" said Roo excitedly. "Maybe we could all use brooms and *sweep* the fog away."

"Say, Roo Boy, that's a fantasterisk idea," said Tigger. "You got any extra-tey brooms there, Piglet?"

"This is my only one," Piglet replied. "But there *is* someone who has lots of brooms."

"Rabbit!" they all yelled together.

Everyone hurried over to Rabbit's house.

"Hey there, Long Ears," Tigger called. "Do you have some brooms we can use?"

Rabbit got excited when he saw all his friends. "A cleaning party?" he exclaimed. "What an excellent idea!"

But, to Rabbit's surprise, everyone took the brooms *outside*.

Rabbit went to see what his friends were doing.

"Oh no, no, no, no!" said Rabbit, watching his brooms in action. "What is going on here?"

"We're sweeping the fog away so that Owl can fly," explained Roo.

"That's silly," said Rabbit. "The fog will go away by itself."

Pooh kept sweeping. "It seems to be getting a bit warmer," he said, wiping his brow.

"I don't need this anymore," said Roo, removing his scarf.

"It's posilutely drier than it was before," noticed Tigger. "I'm not feelin' so wet behind the ears, or anywhere else!"

Roo waited and watched for the fog to leave.

"Why is the day still gray?" he asked, looking around.

"Wait and see," said Rabbit. "As the air warms up more and more, the fog will disappear. Then the day won't be gray anymore."

A few hours later, the only clouds Owl and his friends could see were in the sky.

"What do you know!" announced Owl who was perched atop Rabbit's weather vane. "Rabbit was right! The warmer air has turned this gray, foggy day into a clear one. It's flying weather after all. Thank you all for your help! I'm off to the party. Goodbye!"

Fog in a Jar

Fog is made up of tiny water droplets, which is why Tigger got all wet when he bounced into the fog. Water is always in the air around us, even on a clear day, as an invisible, wispy vapor. When cool air from down low mixes with warm air from up above, we get fog. That is because warm air holds a lot of that wispy vapor. As the temperature rises and the air gets warmer, the water vapor evaporates or disappears, and so does the fog.

Young children learn from doing simple experiments where they can see immediate results!

Make your very own Hundred-Acre Wood fog with this simple experiment.

You will need the following :
- A large jar
- Water
- A strainer
- Some ice cubes

Step 1: Fill the jar with hot water. (Make sure an adult helps you.)

Step 2: Pour out all the water, except for about an inch.

Step 3: Place the strainer over the mouth of the jar and put some ice cubes into it. Now the cold air from the ice cubes mixes with the warm, moist air in the jar. Watch as your Hundred-Acre Wood fog appears!